PILL BUG
DOES NOT NEED ANYBODY

For Pendy, Coco, and Flo,

kind friends to all Pill Bugs—J. F.

SIMON SPOTLIGHT
An imprint of Simon & Schuster Children's Publishing Division
1230 Avenue of the Americas, New York, New York 10020
This Simon Spotlight edition December 2021
Text and illustrations copyright © 2021 by Jonathan Fenske
SIMON SPOTLIGHT, READY-TO-READ, and colophon are registered
trademarks of Simon & Schuster, Inc.
For information about special discounts for bulk purchases, please contact
Simon & Schuster Special Sales at 1-866-506-1949
or business@simonandschuster.com.
Manufactured in the United States of America 1121 LAK
2 4 6 8 10 9 7 5 3 1
Library of Congress Cataloging-in-Publication Data
Names: Fenske, Jonathan, author, illustrator.
Title: Pill Bug does not need anybody / by Jonathan Fenske.
Description: New York: Simon Spotlight, 2021. | Series: Ready-to-read. Pre-level 1 |
Audience: Ages 3–5. | Summary: An independent pill bug learns that sometimes a friend is necessary.
Identifiers: LCCN 2021016681 (print) | LCCN 2021016682 (ebook) | ISBN 9781665900683 (hc) |
ISBN 9781665900676 (pbk) | ISBN 9781665900690 (ebook)
Subjects: CYAC: Self-reliance—Fiction. | Friendship—Fiction. | Wood lice (Crustaceans)—Fiction.
Classification: LCC PZ7.F34843 Pi 2021 (print) | LCC PZ7.F34843 (ebook) | DDC [E]—dc23
LC record available at https://lccn.loc.gov/2021016681

PILL BUG
DOES NOT NEED ANYBODY

BY JONATHAN FENSKE

Ready-to-Read

Simon Spotlight

New York   London   Toronto   Sydney   New Delhi

I am Pill Bug.

I roll alone.

I do not need
ANYBODY.

And I like it
that way.

Watch me roll!

I am happy and free!

Oops.

This is not good.

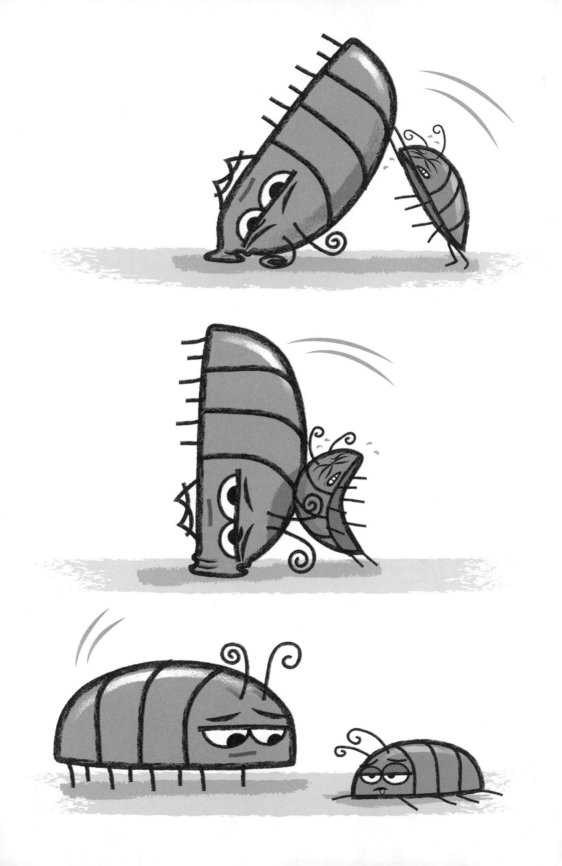

Thanks.

I am Pill Bug.

I swing alone.

I do not need ANYBODY.
And I like it that way.

Watch me swing!
I can swing so high!

Well, maybe not
THAT high.

Thanks. . . .

I am Pill Bug.

I seesaw alone.

I do not need ANYBODY.
And I like it that way.

Watch me seesaw!
Seesawing is FUN.

Okay. This is not fun at all.

I guess I cannot

seesaw alone.

Thanks!

We are Pill Bugs.

We roll together.

And we like it that way.

Because sometimes . . .

We all need somebody.